B
Q

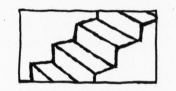

T. CORAGHESSAN BOYLE

She Wasn't Soft

A
BLOOMSBURY
QUID

This story first appeared in the *New Yorker*,
September 1995

First published in Great Britain 1996

Copyright © 1996 by T. Coraghessan Boyle

The moral right of the author has been asserted

Bloomsbury Publishing Plc,
2 Soho Square, London W1V 6HB

A CIP catalogue record for this book
is available from the British Library

ISBN 0 7475 2890 X

Typeset by Hewer Text Composition Services,
Edinburgh
Printed by St Edmundsbury Press, Suffolk
Jacket design by Jeff Fisher

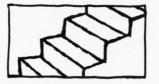

She wasn't tender, she wasn't soft, she wasn't sweetly yielding or coquettish, and she was nobody's little woman and never would be. That had been her mother's role, and look at the sad sack of neuroses and alcoholic dysfunction *she'd* become. And her father. He'd been the pasha of the living room, the sultan of the kitchen, and the emperor of the bedroom, and what had it got him? A stab in the chest, a tender liver, and two feet that might as well have been stumps. Paula Turk wasn't born for that sort of life, with its domestic melodrama and greedy sucking babies – no, she was destined for something richer and more complex, something that would define and elevate her, something great. She wanted to compete and she wanted to win – always shining before her like some numinous icon was the glittering image of triumph. And whenever she flagged, whenever a sniffle or the flu ate at her reserves and she hit the wall in the numbing waters of the Pacific or the devilish winds at the top of San Marcos Pass, she pushed herself through it, drove herself with an internal whip that accepted no excuses and made no allowances for the limitations of the flesh. She was twenty-eight years old and she was going to conquer the world.

On the other hand, Jason Barre, the thirty-three-year-old surf-and-dive-shop proprietor she'd been seeing pretty steadily over the past nine months, didn't really seem to have the fire of competition in him. Both his parents were doctors (and that, as much as anything, had swayed Paula in his favour when they first met), and they'd set him up in his own business, a business that had continuously lost money since its grand opening three years ago.

When the waves were breaking, Jason would be at the beach, and when the surf was flat he'd be stationed behind the counter on his tall swivel stool, selling wax remover to bleached-out adolescents who said things like 'gnarly' and 'killer' in their penetrating, adenoidal tones. Jason liked to surf and he liked to breathe the cigarette haze in sports bars, a permanent sleepy-eyed, widemouthed Californian grin on his face, flip-flops on his feet, and his waist encircled by a pair of faded baggy shorts barely held in place by the gentle sag of his belly and the twin anchors of his hipbones.

That was all right with Paula. She told him he should quit smoking, cut down on his drinking, but she didn't harp on it. In truth, she really didn't care all that much – one world-beater in a relationship was enough. When she was in training, which was all the time now, she couldn't help feeling a kind of moral superiority to anyone who wasn't – and Jason most emphatically wasn't. He was no

threat and he didn't want to be – his mind just
didn't work that way. He was cute, that was all,
and just as she got a little *frisson* of pleasure from
the swell of his paunch beneath the oversized
T-shirt and his sleepy eyes and his laid-back
ways, he admired her for her drive and the lean,
hard triumph of her beauty and her strength.
She never took drugs or alcohol – or hardly
ever – but he persuaded her to try just a puff or
two of marijuana before they made love, and it
seemed to relax her, open up her pores till she
could feel her nerve ends poking through
them, and their lovemaking was like nothing
she'd ever experienced, except maybe breaking
the tape at the end of the twenty-six miles of
the marathon.

It was a Friday night in August, half-past
seven, the sun hanging in the window like a
piñata, and she'd just stepped out of the shower
after a six-hour tuneup for Sunday's triathlon,
when the phone rang. Jason's voice came over
the wire, low and soft. 'Hey, babe,' he said,

breathing into the phone like a sex maniac. (He always called her 'babe', and she loved it, precisely because she wasn't a babe and never would be – it was their little way of mocking the troglodytes moulded into the barstools beside him.)

'Listen, I was just wondering if you might want to join me down at Clubber's for a while. Yeah, I know, you need your sleep and the big day's the day after tomorrow and Zinny Bauer's probably already asleep, but how about it? Come on. It's my birthday.'

'Your birthday? I thought your birthday was in December?'

There was the ghost of a pause during which she could detect the usual wash of background noise, drunken voices crying out as if from the netherworld, the competing announcers of the six different games unfolding simultaneously on the twelve big-screen TVs, the insistent pulse of the jukebox thumping faintly beneath it all. 'No,' he said, 'my birthday's today,

August 26th – it is. I don't know when you got the idea it was in December . . . But come on, babe, don't you have to load up on carbohydrates?'

She did. She admitted it. 'I was going to make pancakes and penne,' she said, 'with a little cheese sauce and maybe a loaf of that brown-and-serve bread . . .'

'I'll take you to the Pasta Bowl, all you can eat – and I swear I'll have you back by eleven.' He lowered his voice. 'And no sex, I know – I wouldn't want to drain you or anything.'

She wasn't soft because she ran forty-five miles a week, biked two hundred and fifty, and slashed through fifteen thousand metres of the crawl in the Baños del Mar pool. She was in the best shape of her life, and Saturday's triathlon was nothing, way less than half the total distance of the big one – the Hawaii Ironman – in October. She wasn't soft because she'd finished second in the women's division last year in Hawaii and forty-fourth over all, beating out one thousand, three hundred and fifty other contestants, twelve hundred of whom, give or take a few, were men. Like Jason. Only fitter. A whole lot fitter.

She swung by Clubber's to pick him up – he wasn't driving, not since his last DUI, anyway – and, though parking was no problem, she had to endure the stench of cigarettes and the faint sour odour of yesterday's vomit while he finished his cocktail and wrapped up his ongoing analysis of the Dodgers' chances with an abstract point about a blister on somebody or other's middle finger. The guy they called Little Drake, white-haired at thirty-six and with a face that reminded Paula of one of those naked drooping dogs, leaned out of his Hawaiian shirt and into the radius of Jason's gesticulating hands as if he'd never heard such wisdom in his life. And Paula? She stood there at the bar in her shorts and Lycra halter top, sucking an Evian through a straw while the sports fans furtively admired her pecs and lats and the hard-hammered musculature of her legs, for all the world a babe. She didn't mind. In fact, it made her feel luminous and alive, not to mention vastly superior to all those pale lumps of flesh sprouting out of the corners like toadstools and the sagging abrasive girlfriends who hung on their arms and tried to feign interest in whatever sport happened to be on the tube.

But somebody was talking to her – Little Drake, it was Little Drake, leaning across Jason and addressing her as if she were one of them. 'So, Paula,' he was saying. 'Paula?'

She swivelled her head toward him, hungry now, impatient. She didn't want to hang around the bar and schmooze about Tommy Lasorda and O.J. and Proposition 187 and how Phil Aguirre had broken both legs and his collarbone in the surf at Rincon; she wanted to go to the Pasta Bowl and carbo-load. 'Yes?' she said, trying to be civil, for Jason's sake.

'You going to put them to shame on Saturday, or what?'

Jason was snubbing out his cigarette in the ashtray, collecting his money from the bar. They were on their way out the door – in ten minutes she'd be forking up fettuccine or angel hair with black olives and sun-dried tomatoes while Jason regaled her with a satiric portrait of his day and all the crazies who'd passed through his shop. This little man with the white hair didn't require a dissertation, and, besides, he couldn't begin to appreciate the difference between what she was doing and the ritualistic farce of the tobacco-spitting, crotch-grabbing 'athletes' all tricked out in their pretty unblemished uniforms up on the screen over his head, so she just smiled, like a babe, and said, 'Yeah.'

Truly, the race was nothing, just a warmup, and it would have been less than nothing but for the puzzling fact that Zinny Bauer was competing. Zinny was a professional, from Hamburg, and she was the one who'd cranked past Paula like some sort of machine in the final stretch of the Ironman last year. What Paula couldn't fathom was why Zinny was bothering with this small-time event when there were so many other plums out there. On the way out of Clubber's, she mentioned it to Jason. 'Not that I'm worried,' she said, 'just mystified.'

It was a fine, soft, glowing night, the air rich with the smell of the surf, the sun squeezing the last light out of the sky as it sank toward Hawaii. Jason was wearing his faded-to-pink 49ers jersey and a pair of shorts so big they made his legs look like sticks. He gave her one of his hooded looks, then got distracted and tapped at his watch twice before lifting it to his ear and frowning. 'Damn thing stopped,' he said. It wasn't until they were sliding into the car that he came back to the subject of Zinny Bauer. 'It's simple, babe,' he said, shrugging his shoulders and letting his face go slack. 'She's here to psych you out.'

He liked to watch her eat. She wasn't shy about it – not like the other girls he'd dated, the ones on a perpetual diet who made you feel like a two-headed hog every time you sat down to a meal, whether it was a Big Mac or the Mexican Plate at La Fondita. No 'salad with dressing on the side' for Paula, no butterless bread or child's portions. She attacked her food like a lumberjack, and you'd better keep your hands and fingers clear. Tonight she started with potato gnocchi in a white sauce puddled with butter, and she ate half a loaf of crusty Italian bread with it, sopping up the left-over sauce till the plate gleamed. Next it was the fettuccine with Alfredo sauce, and on her third trip to the pasta bar she heaped her plate with mostaccioli marinara and chunks of hot sausage – and more bread, always more bread.

He ordered a beer, lit a cigarette without

thinking, and shovelled up some spaghetti carbonara, thick on the fork and sloppy with sauce. The next thing he knew, he was staring up into the hot green gaze of the waitperson, a pencil-necked little fag he could have snapped in two like a breadstick if this weren't California and everything so copacetic and laid-back. It was times like this when he wished he lived in Cleveland, even though he'd never been there, but he knew what was coming and he figured people in Cleveland wouldn't put up with this sort of crap.

'You'll have to put that out,' the little fag said.

'Sure, man,' Jason said, gesturing broadly so that the smoke fanned out around him like the remains of a pissed-over fire. 'Just as soon as I' – puff, puff – 'take another drag and' – puff, puff – 'find me an ashtray somewhere . . . you wouldn't happen' – puff, puff – 'to have an ashtray, would you?'

Of course the little fag had been holding one

out in front of him all along, as if it were a portable potty or something, but the cigarette was just a glowing stub now, the tiny fag end of a cigarette – fag end, how about that? – and Jason reached out, crushed the thing in the ashtray and said, 'Hey, thanks, dude – even though it really wasn't a cigarette but just the *fag* end of one.'

And then the waiter was gone and Paula was there, her fourth plate of the evening mounded high with angel hair, three-bean salad, and wedges of fruit in five different colours. 'So what was that all about? Your cigarette?'

Jason ignored her, forking up spaghetti. He took a long swig of his beer and shrugged. 'Yeah, whatever,' he said finally. 'One more fascist doing his job.'

'Don't be like that,' she said, using the heel of her bread to chase the beans around the plate.

'Like what?'

'You know what I mean. I don't have to lecture you.'

'Yeah?' He let his eyes droop. 'So what do you call this, then?'

She sighed and looked away, and that sigh really irritated him, rankled him, made him feel like flipping the table over and sailing a few plates through the window. He was drunk. Or three-quarters drunk, anyway. Then her lips were moving again. 'Everybody in the world doesn't necessarily enjoy breathing through a tube of incinerated tobacco, you know,' she said. 'People are into health.'

'Who? You maybe. But the rest of them just want to be a pain in the ass. They just want to abrogate my rights in a public place' – abrogate, now where did that come from? – 'and then rub my nose in it.' The thought soured him even more, and when he caught the waitperson pussyfooting by out of the corner of his eye he snapped his fingers with as much

16

pure malice as he could manage. 'Hey, dude, another beer here, huh? I mean, when you get a chance.'

It was then that Zinny Bauer made her appearance. She stalked through the door like something crossbred in an experimental laboratory, so rangy and hollow-eyed and fleshless she looked as if she'd been pasted on to her bones. There was a guy with her – her trainer or husband or whatever – and he was right out of an X-Men cartoon, all head and shoulders and great big beefy biceps. Jason recognised them from Houston – he'd flown down to watch Paula compete in the Houston race only to see her hit the wall in the run and finish sixth in the women's while Zinny Bauer, the Amazing Bone Woman, took an easy first. And here they were, Zinny and Klaus – or Olaf, or whoever – here in the Pasta Bowl, carbo-loading like anybody else. His beer came, cold and dependable, green in the bottle, pale amber in the glass, and he downed it in two gulps. 'Hey, Paula,' he said, and he couldn't keep the quick sharp stab of joy out of his voice – he was happy suddenly and he didn't know why. 'Hey, Paula, you see who's here?'

The thing that upset her was that he'd lied to her, the way her father used to lie to her mother, the same way – casually, almost as a reflex. It wasn't his birthday at all. He'd just said that to get her out because he was drunk and he didn't care if she had to compete the day after tomorrow and needed her rest and peace and quiet and absolutely no stimulation whatever. He was selfish, that was all, selfish and un-thinking. And then there was the business with the cigarette – he knew as well as anybody in the state that there was an ordinance against smoking in public places as of January last, and still he had to push the limits like some cocky immature chip-on-the-shoulder surfer. Which is exactly what he was. But all that was forgivable – it was the Zinny Bauer business she just couldn't forgive.

Paula wasn't even supposed to be there. She was supposed to be at home, making up a batch of pancakes and penne with cheese sauce and lying inert on the couch with the remote control. This was the night before the night before the event, a time to fuel up her tanks and veg out. But because of him, because of her silver-tongued hero in the baggy shorts, she was at the Pasta Bowl, carbo-loading in public. And so was Zinny Bauer, the last person on earth she wanted to see.

That was bad enough, but Jason made it worse, far worse – Jason made it into one of the most excruciating moments of her life. What happened was purely crazy and if she didn't know Jason better she would have thought he'd planned it. They were squabbling over his cigarette and how unlaid-back and uptight the whole thing had made him – he was drunk, and she didn't appreciate him when he was drunk, not at all – when his face suddenly took on a conspiratorial look and he said, 'Hey, Paula, you see who's here?'

'Who?' she said, and she shot a glance over her shoulder and froze: it was Zinny Bauer and her husband, Armin. 'Oh, shit,' she said, and she lowered her head and focused on her plate as if it were the most fascinating thing she'd ever seen. 'She didn't see me, did she? We've got to go. Right now. Right this minute.'

Jason was smirking. He looked happy about it, as if he and Zinny Bauer were old friends. 'But you've only had four plates, babe,' he said. 'You sure we got our money's worth? I could go for maybe just a touch more pasta – and I haven't even had any salad yet.'

'No joking around, this isn't funny.' Her voice withered in her throat. 'I don't want to see her. I don't want to talk to her. I just want to get out of here, OK?'

His smile got wider. 'Sure, babe, I know how you feel – but you're going to beat her, you are, no sweat. You don't have to let anybody chase you out of your favourite restaurant in your own town – I mean, that's not right, is it? That's not in the spirit of friendly competition.'

'Jason,' she said, and she reached across the table and took hold of his wrist. 'I mean it. Let's get out of here. Now.'

Her throat was constricted, everything she'd eaten about to come up. Her legs ached, and her ankle – the one she'd sprained last spring – felt as if someone had driven a nail through it. All she could think of was Zinny Bauer, with her long muscles and the shaved blonde stubble of her head and her eyes that never quit. Zinny Bauer was behind her, at her back, right there, and it was too much to bear. '*Jason*,' she hissed.

'OK, OK,' he was saying, and he tipped back the dregs of his beer and reached into his pocket and scattered a couple of rumpled bills across the table to cover the checks. Then he rose from the chair with a slow drunken grandeur and gave her a wink as if to indicate that the coast was clear. She got up, hunching her shoulders as if she could compress herself into invisibility, and stared down at her feet as Jason took her arm and led her across the room – if Zinny saw her, Paula wouldn't know about it, because she wasn't going to look up and she wasn't going to make eye contact, she wasn't.

Or so she thought.

She was concentrating on her feet, on the black-and-white-checked pattern of the floor tiles and how her running shoes negotiated them as if they were attached to somebody else's legs, when all of a sudden Jason stopped and her eyes flew up and she saw that they were hovering over Zinny Bauer's table like casual acquaintances, like neighbours on their way to a PTA meeting. 'But aren't you Zinny Bauer?' Jason said, his voice gone high and nasal as he shifted into his Valley Girl imitation. 'The great triathlete? Oh God, yes, yes, you are, aren't you? Oh, God, could I have your autograph for my little girl?'

Paula was made of stone. She couldn't move, couldn't speak, couldn't even blink her eyes. And Zinny – she looked as if her plane had just crashed. Jason was playing out the charade, pretending to fumble through his pockets for a pen, when Armin broke the silence. 'Why don't you just fock off,' he said, and the veins stood out in his neck.

'Oh, she'll be so thrilled,' Jason went on, his voice pinched to a squeal. 'She's so adorable, only six years old, and, oh my God, she's not going to believe this!'

Armin rose to his feet. Zinny clutched at the edge of the table with bloodless fingers, her eyes narrow and hard. The waiter – the one Jason had been riding – started toward them, crying out, 'Is everything all right?' as if the phrase had any meaning.

And then Jason's voice changed, just like that. 'Fuck you, too, Jack, and your scrawny fucking bald-headed squeeze.'

Armin worked out, you could see that, and

23

SHE WASN'T SOFT

Paula doubted he'd ever pressed a cigarette to his lips, let alone a joint, but still Jason managed to hold his own – at least until the kitchen staff separated them. There was some breakage, a couple of chairs overturned, a whole lot of noise and cursing and threatening, most of it from Jason. Every face in the restaurant was drained of colour by the time the kitchen staff came to the rescue, and somebody went to the phone and called the police, but Jason blustered his way out the door and disappeared before they arrived. And Paula? She just melted away and kept on melting until she found herself behind the wheel of the car, cruising slowly down the darkened streets, looking for Jason.

She never did find him.

When he called the next morning, he was all sweetness and apology. He whispered, moaned, sang to her, his voice a continuous soothing current insinuating itself through the line and into her head and right on down

through her veins and arteries to the unresist-
ing core of her. 'Listen, Paula, I didn't mean for
things to get out of hand,' he whispered,
'you've got to believe me. I just didn't think
you had to hide from anybody, that's all.'

She listened, her mind gone numb, and let
his words saturate her. It was the day before the
event, and she wasn't going to let anything
distract her. But then, as he went on, pouring
himself into the phone with his penitential,
self-pitying tones as if he were the one who'd
been embarrassed and humiliated, she felt the
outrage coming up in her: didn't he under-
stand, didn't he know what it meant to stare
into the face of your own defeat? And over a
plate of pasta, no less? She cut him off in the
middle of a long digression about some surfing
legend of the fifties and all the adversity he'd
had to face from a host of competitors, a blood-
sucking wife, and a fearsome backwash off
Newport Beach.

'What did you think?' she demanded. 'That

you were protecting me or something? Is that it? Because if that's what you think, let me tell you I don't need you or anybody else to stand up for me – '

'Paula,' he said, his voice creeping out at her over the wire, 'Paula – I'm on your side, remember? I love what you're doing. I want to help you.' He paused. 'And yes, I want to protect you, too.'

'I don't need it.'

'Yes, you do. You don't think you do, but you do. Don't you see: I was trying to psych her.'

'Psych her? At the Pasta Bowl?'

His voice was soft, so soft she could barely hear him: 'Yeah.' And then, even softer: 'I did it for you.'

It was Saturday, seventy-eight degrees, sun beaming down unmolested, the tourists out in force. The shop had been buzzing since ten, nothing major – cords, tube socks, T-shirts, a couple of illustrated guides to South Coast hot spots that nobody who knew anything needed a book to find – but Jason had been at the cash register right through lunch and on into the four-thirty breathing spell, when the tourist mind tended to fixate on ice-cream cones and those pathetic sidecar bikes they pedalled up and down the street like the true guppies they were. He'd even called Little Drake in to help out for a couple of hours there. Drake didn't mind. He'd grown up rich in Montecito and gone white-haired at twenty-seven, and now he lived with his even whiter-haired old parents and managed their two rental properties downtown – which meant he had nothing much to do except prop up the bar at Clubber's or haunt the shop like the thinnest ghost of a customer. So why not put him to work?

'Nothing to shout about,' Jason told him, over the faint hum of the oldies channel. He leaned back against the wall on his high stool and cracked the first beer of the day. 'Little stuff, but a lot of it. I almost had that one dude sold on the Al Merrick board – I could taste it – but something scared him off. Maybe Mommy took away his Visa card, I don't know.'

Drake pulled contemplatively at his beer and looked out the window at the parade of tourists marching up and down State Street. He didn't respond. It was approaching that crucial hour of the day, the hour known as cocktail hour, two for one, the light struck on the underside of the palms, everything soft and pretty and winding down toward dinner and evening, the whole night held out before them like a promise. 'What time's the Dodger game?' Drake said finally.

Jason looked at his watch. It was a reflex. The Dodgers were playing the Pods at five-thirty, Nomo against Benes, and he knew the time and channel as well as he knew his ATM number. The Angels were on Prime Ticket, seven-thirty, at home against the Orioles. And Paula – Paula was at home, too, focusing (do not disturb, thank you very much) for the big one with the Amazing Bone Woman the next morning. 'Five-thirty,' he said, after a long pause.

Drake said nothing. His beer was gone, and he shuffled behind the counter to the little reefer for another. When he'd cracked it, sipped, belched, scratched himself thoroughly, and commented on the physique of an over-weight Mexican chick in a red bikini making her way up from the beach, he ventured a query on the topic under consideration: 'Time to close up?'

All things being equal, Jason would have stayed open till six, or near six anyway, on a Saturday in August. The summer months accounted for the lion's share of his business – it was like the Christmas season for everybody else – and he tried to maximise it, he really did, but he knew what Drake was saying. Twenty to five now, and they still had to count the receipts, lock up, stop by the night deposit at the B. of A., and then settle in at Clubber's for the game. It would be nice to be there, maybe with a tall tequila tonic and the sports section spread out on the bar, before the game got under way. Just to settle in and enjoy the fruits of their labour. He gave a sigh, for form's sake, and said, 'Yeah, why not?'

And then there was cocktail hour, and he had a couple of tall tequila tonics before switching to beer, and the Dodgers looked good, real good, red hot, and somebody bought him a shot. Drake was carrying on about something – his girlfriend's cat, the calluses on his mother's feet – and Jason tuned him out, ordered two soft chicken tacos and watched the sun do all sorts of amazing pink-and-salmon things to the store-fronts across the street before the grey finally settled in. He was thinking he should have gone surfing today, thinking he'd maybe go out in the morning, and then he was thinking of Paula. He should wish her luck or something, give her a phone call, at least. But the more he thought about it, the more he pictured her alone in her apartment power-drinking her fluids, sunk into the shell of her focus like some Chinese Zen master, and the more he wanted to see her.

They hadn't had sex in a week. She was always like that when it was coming down to the wire, and he didn't blame her. Or yes – yes, he did blame her. And he resented it, too. What was the big deal? It wasn't like she was playing ball or anything that took any skill – and why lock him out for that? She was like his overachieving, straight-arrow parents, Type A personalities, early risers, joggers, let's go out and beat the world. God, that was anal. But she had some body on her, as firm and flawless as the Illustrated Man's – or Woman's, actually. He thought about that and about the way her face softened when they were in bed together, and he stood at the pay phone seeing her in the hazy soft-focus glow of some made-for-TV movie. Maybe he shouldn't call. Maybe he should just . . . surprise her.

She answered the door in an oversized sweatshirt and shorts, barefooted, and with the half-full pitcher from the blender in her hand. She looked surprised, all right, but not pleasantly surprised. In fact, she scowled at him and set the pitcher down on the bookcase before pulling back the door and ushering him in. He didn't even get the chance to tell her he loved her or to wish her luck before she started in on him. 'What are you doing here?' she demanded. 'You know I can't see you tonight, of all nights. What's with you? Are you drunk? Is that it?'

What could he say? He stared at the brown gloop in the pitcher for half a beat and then gave her his best simmering droopy-eyed smile and a shrug that radiated down from his shoulders to his hips. 'I just wanted to see you. To wish you luck, you know?' He stepped forward to kiss her, but she dodged away from him, snatching up the pitcher full of gloop like a shield. 'A kiss for luck?' he said.

She hesitated. He could see something go in and out of her eyes, the flicker of a worry, competitive anxiety, butterflies, and then she smiled and pecked him a kiss on the lips that tasted of soy and honey and whatever else was in that concoction she drank. 'Luck,' she said, 'but no excitement.'

'And no sex,' he said, trying to make a joke of it. 'I know.'

She laughed then, a high, girlish tinkle of a laugh that broke the spell. 'No sex,' she said. 'But I was just going to watch a movie, if you want to join me – '

He found one of the beers he'd left in the refrigerator for just such an emergency as this and settled in beside her on the couch to watch the movie – some inspirational crap about a demi-cripple who wins the hurdle event in the Swedish Special Olympics – but he was hot, he couldn't help it, and his fingers kept wandering

33

from her shoulder to her breast, from her waist to her inner thigh. At least she kissed him when she pushed him away. 'Tomorrow,' she promised, but it was only a promise, and they both knew it. She'd been so devastated after the Houston thing she wouldn't sleep with him for a week and a half, strung tight as a bow every time he touched her. The memory of it chewed at him, and he sipped his beer moodily. 'Bullshit,' he said.

'Bullshit what?'

'Bullshit you'll sleep with me tomorrow. Remember Houston? Remember Zinny Bauer?'

Her face changed suddenly and she flicked the remote angrily at the screen and the picture went blank. 'I think you'd better go,' she said.

But he didn't want to go. She was his girlfriend, wasn't she? And what good did it do him if she kicked him out every time some chickenshit race came up? Didn't he matter to

34

her, didn't he matter at all? 'I don't want to go,' he said.

She stood, put her hands on her hips, and glared at him. 'I have to go to bed now.'

He didn't budge. Didn't move a muscle. 'That's what I mean,' he said, and his face was ugly, he couldn't help it. 'I want to go to bed, too.'

Later, he felt bad about the whole thing. Worse than bad. He didn't know how it happened exactly, but there was some resentment there, he guessed, and it just snuck up on him – plus he was drunk, if that was any excuse. Which it wasn't. Anyway, he hadn't meant to get physical, and by the time she'd stopped fighting him and he got her shorts down he hadn't even really wanted to go through with it. This wasn't making love, this wasn't what he wanted. She just lay there beneath him like she was dead, like some sort of zombie, and it made him sick, so sick he couldn't even begin to apologise or excuse himself. He felt her eyes on him as he was zipping up, hard eyes, accusatory eyes, eyes like claws, and he had to stagger into the bathroom and cover himself with the noise of both taps and the toilet to keep from breaking down. He'd gone too far. He knew it. He was ashamed of himself, deeply ashamed, and there really wasn't anything left to say. He just slumped his shoulders and slouched out the door.

And now here he was, contrite and hung over, mooning around on East Beach in the cool hush of 7 a.m., waiting with all the rest of the guppies for the race to start. Paula wouldn't even look at him. Her mouth was set, clamped shut, a tiny little line of nothing beneath her nose, and her eyes looked no further than her equipment – her spidery ultra-lightweight bike with the triathlon bars and her little skullcap of a helmet and water bottles and whatnot. She was wearing a two-piece swimsuit, and she'd already had her number – 23 – painted on her upper arms and the long burnished muscles of her thighs. He shook out a cigarette and stared off past her, wondering what they used for the numbers – Magic Marker? Greasepaint? Something that wouldn't come off in the surf, anyway – or with all the sweat. He remembered the way she'd looked in Houston, pounding through the muggy haze in a sheen of sweat, her face sunk in a mask of suffering, her legs and buttocks taut, her breasts flattened to her chest in the grip of the clinging top. He thought about that, watching her from behind the police line as she bent to fool with her bike, not an ounce of fat on her, nothing, not even a stray hair, and he got hard just looking at her.

But that was short-lived, because he felt bad about last night and knew he'd really have to put himself through the wringer to make it up to her. Plus, just watching the rest of the four hundred and six fleshless masochists parade by with their Gore-Tex T-shirts and Lycra shorts and all the rest of their paraphernalia was enough to make him go cold all over. His stomach felt like a fried egg left out on the counter too long, and his hands shook when he lit the cigarette. He should be in bed, that's where he should be – enough of this 7 a.m. They were crazy, these people, purely crazy, getting up at dawn to put themselves through something like this – one mile in the water, thirty-four on the bike, and a ten-mile run to wrap it up, and this was a walk compared to the Ironman. They were all bone and long lean muscle, like whippet dogs or something, the women indistinguishable from the men, stringy and titless. Except for Paula. She was all right in that department, and that was genetic – she referred to her breasts as her fat reserves. He was wondering if they shrank at all during the race, what with all that stress and water loss, when a woman with big hair and too much make-up asked him for a light.

She was milling around with maybe a couple of hundred other spectators – or sadists, he

guessed you'd have to call them – waiting to
watch the crazies do their thing. 'Thanks,' she
breathed, after he'd leaned in close to touch the
tip of his smoke to hers. Her eyes were big wet
pools, and she was no freak, no bone woman.
Her lips were wet, too, or maybe it was his
imagination. 'So,' she said, the voice caught
low in her throat, a real smoker's rasp, 'here for
the big event?'

He just nodded.

There was a pause. They sucked at their
cigarettes. A pair of gulls flailed sharply at the
air behind them and then settled down to poke
through the sand for anything that looked
edible. 'My name's Sandra,' she offered, but
he wasn't listening, not really, because it was
then that it came to him, his inspiration, his
moment of grace and redemption: suddenly, he
knew how he was going to make it up to Paula.
He cut his eyes away from the woman and
through the crowd to where Paula bent over
her equipment, the take-no-prisoners look

ironed into her face. And what does she want more than anything? he asked himself, his excitement so intense he almost spoke the words aloud. What would make her happy, glad to see him, ready to party, celebrate, dance till dawn, and let bygones be bygones?

To win. That was all. To beat Zinny Bauer. And in that moment, even as Paula caught his eye and glowered at him, he had a vision of Zinny Bauer, the Amazing Bone Woman, coming into the final stretch with her legs and arms pumping, in command, no problem, and the bright-green cup of Gatorade held out for her by the smiling volunteer in the official volunteer's cap and T-shirt – yes – and Zinny Bauer refreshing herself, drinking it down in mid-stride, running on and on until she hit the wall he was already constructing.

Paula pulled the red bathing cap down over her ears, adjusted her swim goggles, and strode across the beach, her heartbeat as slow and steady as a lizard's on a cold rock. She was focused, as clear-headed and certain as she'd ever been in her life. Nothing mattered now except leaving all the hotshots and loudmouths and macho types behind in the dust – and Zinny Bauer, too. There were a couple of pros competing in the men's division and she had no illusions about beating them, but she was going to teach the rest of them a hard lesson, a lesson about toughness and endurance and will. If anything, what had happened with Jason last night was something she could use, the kind of thing that made her angry, that made her wonder what she'd seen in him in the first place. He didn't care about her. He didn't care about anybody. That was what she was thinking when the gun went off and she hit the water with the great thundering herd of them, the image of his bleary apologetic face burning into her brain – date rape, that's what they called it – and she came out of the surf just behind Zinny Bauer, Jill Eisen, and Tommy Roe, one of the men's pros.

All right, OK. She was on her bike now, through the gate in a flash and driving down the flat wide concourse of Cabrillo Boulevard in perfect rhythm, effortless, as if the blood were flowing through her legs and into the bike itself. Before she'd gone half a mile, she knew she was going to catch Zinny Bauer and pass her to ride with the men's leaders and get off first on the run. It was preordained, she could feel it, feel it pounding in her temples and in the perfect engine of her heart. The anger had settled in her legs now, a bitter, hot-burning fuel. She fed on the air, tucked herself into the handlebars, and flew. If all this time she'd raced for herself, for something uncontainable inside her, now she was racing for Jason, to show him up, to show him what she was, what she really was. There was no excuse for him. None. And she was going to win this event, she was going to beat Zinny Bauer and

all those hundreds of soft, winded, under-
trained, crowing, chest-thumping jocks, too,
and she was going to accept her trophy and
stride right by him as if he didn't exist, because
she wasn't soft, she wasn't, and he was going to
find that out once and for all.

By the time he got back to the beach, Jason
thought he'd run some sort of race himself. He
was breathing hard – got to quit smoking – and
his tequila headache was heating up to the
point where he was seriously considering
ducking into Clubber's and slamming a shot
or two, though it was only half-past nine and all
the tourists would be there, buttering their
French toast and would you pass the syrup,
please, and thank you very much. He'd had to
go all the way out to Drake's place and shake
him awake to get the Tuinol – one of Drake's
mother's six thousand and one prescriptions to
fight off the withering aches of her seventy-
odd years. Tuinol, Nembutal, Dalmane, Dar-

vocet: Jason didn't care, just so long as there was enough of it. He didn't do barbiturates any more – probably hadn't swallowed a Tooey in ten years – but he remembered the sweet numb glow they gave him and the way they made his legs feel like treetrunks planted deep in the ground.

The sun had burned off the fog by now, and the day was clear and glittering on the water. They'd started the race at seven-thirty, so that gave him a while yet – the first men would be crossing the finish line in just under three hours, and the women would be coming in at three-ten, three-twelve, something like that. All he needed to do now was finesse himself into the inner sanctum, pick up a stray T-shirt and cap, find the Gatorade, and plant himself about two miles from the finish. Of course, there was a chance the Amazing Bone Woman wouldn't take the cup from him, especially if she recognised him from the other night, but he was going to pull his cap down low and hide

behind his Ray-Bans and show her a face of
devotion. One second, that's all it would take.
A hand coming out of the crowd, the cup
beaded with moisture and moving right along
beside her so she didn't even have to break
stride – and what was there to think about? She
drinks and hits the wall. And if she didn't go for
it the first time, he'd hop in the car and catch
her a mile farther on.

He'd been watching one of the security
volunteers stationed outside the trailer that
served as a command centre. A kid of eight-
een, maybe, greasy hair, an oversized cross
dangling from one ear, a scurf of residual
acne. He was a carbon copy of the kids he
sold wetsuits and Killer Beeswax to – maybe
he was even one of them. Jason reminded
himself to tread carefully. He was a business-
man, after all, one of the pillars of the downtown community, and somebody might
recognise him. But then so what if they did?
He was volunteering his time, that was all, a

committed citizen doing his civic best to promote tourism and everything else that was right in the world. He ducked under the rope. 'Hey, bro,' he said to the kid, extending his hand for the high five – which the kid gave him. 'Sorry I'm late. Jeff around?'

The kid's face opened up in a big beaming half-witted grin. 'Yeah, sure – I think he went up the beach a ways with Everardo and Linda and some of the press people, but I could maybe look if you want – '

Jeff. It was a safe bet – no crowd of that size, especially one consisting of whippets, bone people, and guppies, would be without a Jeff. Jason gave the kid a shrug. 'Nah, that's all right. But hey, where's the T-shirts and caps at?'

Then he was in his car, and forget the DUI, the big green waxed cup cold between his legs, breaking Tuinol caps and looking for a parking space along the course. He pulled in under a huge Monterey pine that was like its own little city and finished doctoring the Gatorade, stirring the stuff in with his index finger. What would it take to make the Bone Woman's legs go numb and wind up a Did Not Finish without arousing suspicion? Two? Three? He didn't want her to pass out on the spot or take a dive into the bushes or anything, and he didn't want to hurt her, either, not really. But four — four was a nice round number, and that ought to do it. He sucked the finger he'd used as a swizzle stick to see if he could detect the taste, but he couldn't. He took a tentative sip. Nothing. Gatorade tasted like such shit anyway, who could tell the difference?

He found a knot of volunteers in their canary-yellow T-shirts and caps and stationed himself a hundred yards up the street from them, the ice rattling as he swirled his little green time bomb around the lip of the cup. The breeze was soft, the sun caught in the crowns of the trees and reaching out to finger the road here and there in long slim swatches.

47

He'd never tell Paula, of course, no way, but he'd get giddy with her, pop the champagne cork, and let her fill him with all the ecstasy of victory.

A cheer from the crowd brought him out of his reverie. The first of the men was cranking his way around the long bend in the road, a guy with a beard and wraparound sunglasses – the Finn. He was the one favoured to win, or was it the Brit? Jason tucked the cup behind his back and faded into the crowd, which was pretty sparse here, and watched the guy propel himself past, his mouth gaping black, the two holes of his nostrils punched deep into his face, his head bobbing on his neck as if it weren't attached right. Another guy appeared around the corner just as the Finn passed by, and then two others came slogging along behind him. Somebody cheered, but it was a pretty feeble affair.

Jason checked his watch. It would be five minutes or so, and then he could start watching for the Amazing Bone Woman, tireless freak that she was. And did she fuck Klaus, or Olaf, or whoever he was, the night before the big event, or was she like Paula, all focus and negativity and no, no, no? He fingered the cup lightly, reminding himself not to damage or crease it in any way – it had to look pristine, fresh-dipped from the bucket – and he watched the corner at the end of the street till his eyes began to blur from the sheer concentration of it all.

Two more men passed by and nobody cheered, not a murmur, but then suddenly a couple of middle-aged women across the street set up a howl, and the crowd chimed in: the first woman, a woman of string and bone with a puffing heaving puppetlike frame, was swinging into the street in distant silhouette. Jason moved forward. He tugged reflexively at the bill of his hat, jammed the rims of the shades back into his eyesockets. And he started to grin, all his teeth on fire, his lips spread wide: Here, take me, drink me, have me!

As the woman drew closer, loping, sweating, elbows flailing and knees pounding, the crowd getting into it now, cheering her, cheering this first of the women in a man's event, the first Ironwoman of the day, he began to realise that this wasn't Zinny Bauer at all. Her hair was too long, and her legs and chest were too full – and then he saw the number clearly, No. 23, and looked into Paula's face. She was fifty yards from him, but he could see the toughness in her eyes and the tight little frozen smile of triumph and superiority. She was winning. She was beating Zinny Bauer and Jill Eisen and all those pathetic jocks labouring up the hills and down the blacktop streets behind her. This was her moment, this was it.

But then, and he didn't stop to think about it, he stepped forward, right out on the street where she could see him, and held out the cup. He heard her feet beating at the pavement with a hard merciless slap, saw the icy twist of a smile and the cold triumphant eyes. And he felt the briefest fleeting touch of her flesh as the cup left his hand.

A NOTE ON THE AUTHOR

T. Coraghessan Boyle is the author of many novels and collections of short stories. His most recent novel is *The Tortilla Curtain*. He lives in Montecito, California.

AVAILABLE AS BLOOMSBURY CLASSICS